York Boun

Presents:

Shari's Crossing

Written by: R.D. ARCHER

Follow RD ARCHER on Twitter @Passion082

Follow York Bound Publications on Twitter @yorkboundpub

SHARI'S CROSSING is a work of fiction. Names, characters, and events are from the author's imagination or used fictitiously. Any resemblence to actual people or events is purely coincidental.

YORK BOUND PUBLICATIONS

www.yorkboundpublications.com

"THE PAIN OF ONE SOUL HELPED TO FREE ANOTHER SOUL"

CHAPTER-1

I been up since 4:30 this morning getting breakfast started for Ms. Sarah and the kids. *I went out back to the shed to get some eggs and milk from the ice-box. It's still dark outside. I turned to leave to head back to the house only to find massa Willis blocking the door. He took a drag off his cigarette and blew the smoke into the early morning air. I feel sick to my stomach and desperate to leave. I look down at the hay on the shed floor. I can feel the sweat beading on my forehead and my breath quickening. I looked up and massa Willis is right in front of me. I tell myself, don't make him mad. Maybe he will be done fast and maybe he won't hurt me. He say "good morning" to me, but I don't say nothing. I just keep my eyes focused on the floor. He say, "don't you hear me talking to you girl?!" I say "yessuh. I hears fine, and I best be getting inside to start breakfast for Ms. Sarah." He say " Ms. Sarah still sleepin'," and " don't you want to have some fun?" I don't say nothing, and he don't wait for a answer. He push me on the* floor. The eggs and jug of milk shatter on the floor. Massa step on my chest with his boot and take another drag off his cigarette. His eyes was black and empty. And I could swear I was looking at the devil 'hisself'. Massa plucked the cigarette on my arm and start pulling his overalls from his shoulders. He let his pants drop to the floor and kicked them off his feet to the side. Oh lord help me! I don't want him to touch me! He say " open your legs." I don't. I hold tightly to the hem of my dress to keep it down. I say "please massa Willis! Please don't!" He bend over me and rip my dress with both hands, exposing my bare breast and stomach. He pull the rags from my shoulders and grab what's left of my dress from under me. I cross my arms to hide myself. He is just staring at me. He bend down near my face and I can smell the whiskey. He whisper in my ear "Am I going to make this hard?" and "It would be best not to fight." I want to curl up on my side but he push my shoulder back to the floor and slap me in the mouth. He push my legs apart and sticks two, and then three fingers in me. His fingernails scratch the sensitive walls of flesh and draw blood. I just lay there. I can feel me leaving myself. I always leave myself. Massa shoved 'hisself' in me, thrusting hard and fast. I can see me laying there. Tears form a path from the corners of my eyes to a puddle in my ear. My lip is swollen and bleeding, but I don't feel nothing. I'm not there. I can see his breath move the hay on the floor as his breathing becomes more and more labored. He almost done. If I can just yell to Ms. Sarah and wake her up, she can stop him. She can stop this. I need to yell for help, but he'll beat me. He done his business and just lay on me, crushing me with his weight. He slowly pushes 'hisself' up and stands. He kicks me between my open legs before picking up his pants and leaving the shed. I yell out in pain. I cry. I cry. CRY. Cryy.

****

****

"Shari! Shari! Girl wake the hell up! Every damned time I need to get up early, you and those fuckin' nightmares wake me up! It's a wonder somebody hasn't knocked on the door because of all that screaming you be doing! I'm going to sleep in Jessica's room!"

"Oh my gosh Lynn! I'm sorry!" I said trying to catch my breath. Another bad dream. I wiped the tears from my face. This time I'm drenched in sweat. I can't stop my heart from racing.

"Your ass need to go see a doctor about that problem! I'm out!" Lynne said grabbing her pillow and blanket, slamming the door behind her.

I called Neil. I always call Neil after a bad dream. Just talking to him helped ease me back to sleep. Even though it's 2:00 in the morning, Neil will answer for me. He's not only my boyfriend, but he's my best friend. It seems like I've known him my entire life. We started dating during freshman year. We were friends first, but quickly realized that there was a lot more to the friendship. We shared everything with each other.

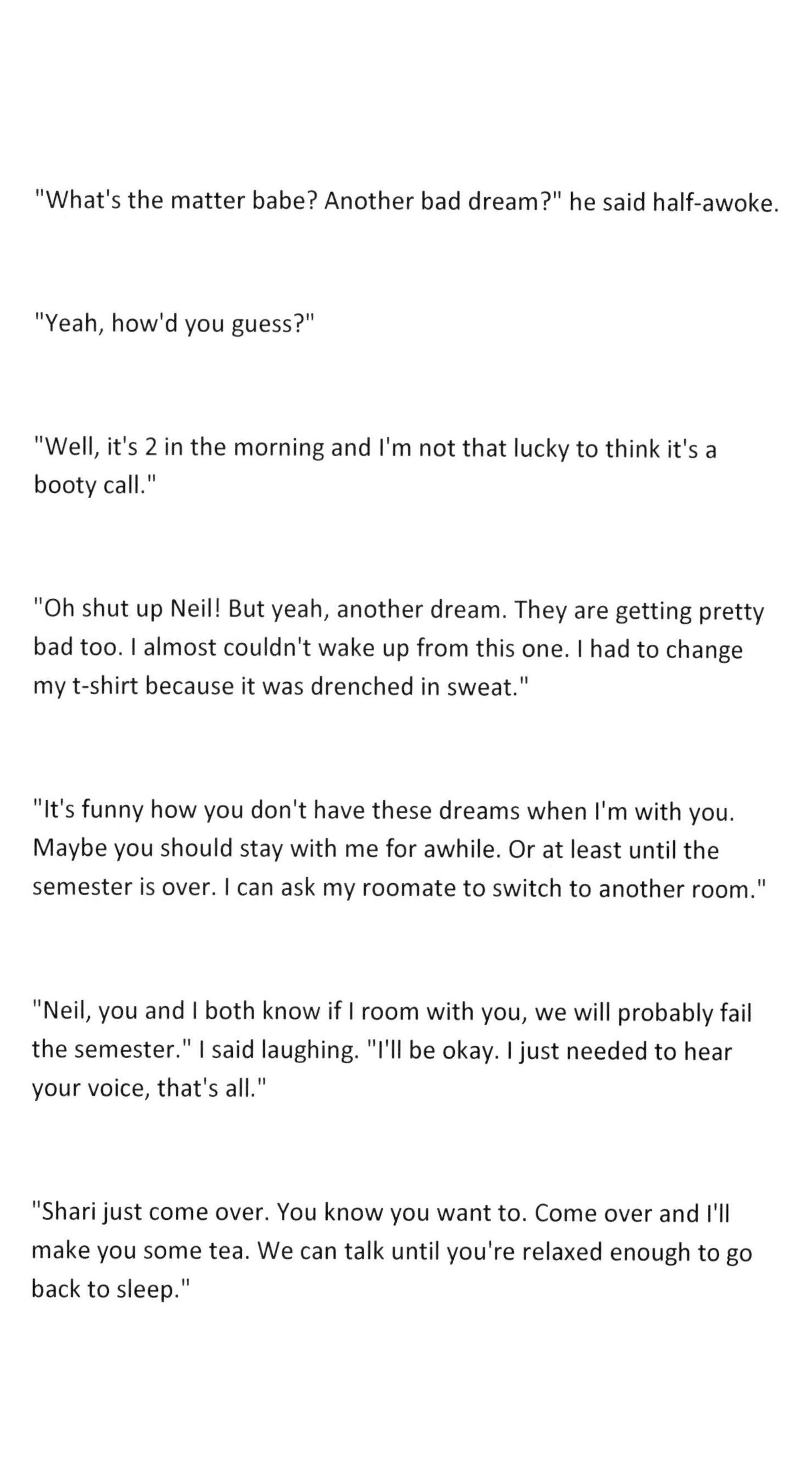

"What's the matter babe? Another bad dream?" he said half-awoke.

"Yeah, how'd you guess?"

"Well, it's 2 in the morning and I'm not that lucky to think it's a booty call."

"Oh shut up Neil! But yeah, another dream. They are getting pretty bad too. I almost couldn't wake up from this one. I had to change my t-shirt because it was drenched in sweat."

"It's funny how you don't have these dreams when I'm with you. Maybe you should stay with me for awhile. Or at least until the semester is over. I can ask my roomate to switch to another room."

"Neil, you and I both know if I room with you, we will probably fail the semester." I said laughing. "I'll be okay. I just needed to hear your voice, that's all."

"Shari just come over. You know you want to. Come over and I'll make you some tea. We can talk until you're relaxed enough to go back to sleep."

"Okay. it is kinda creepy over here since Lynne left. I'll be right down."

I showered quickly and changed into my Victoria Secret yoga shorts, tank-top, and hoodie. I put my braids up into a bun and slid into my flip-flops. I checked myself out in the mirror before grabbing my keys to leave. I loved the way my chocolate skin looked in pink. The yoga shorts hugged my curvy hips and round butt while the tank-top accentuated the plumpness of my breast and the shapeliness of my waist. I wasn't a tiny girl, that's for sure! I had a lot to work with as a beautiful, black woman.

I left my room and headed for the stairs. It was a cool fall night and I could feel the air coming in through the cracks around the windows that lined the hallway. Louisianna University was one of the oldest colleges in town and the campus buildings were a constant reminder of just how old it was. Winston Residence Hall was built in the 1800's and the architecture was untouched. The building was made of gray stone and covered from top to bottom with vines. The windows reached the high ceilings. The bluish glow from the moon became my personal spotlight in the dark hallway. My flip-flops smacked the cold marble tiles as I made my way downstairs to Neil's room.

I loved Neil's room. It was so warm and cozy, but a reflection of him. Neil was 6'3" and nicely built. His eyes were hazelnut brown with thick, dark eyelashes and eyebrows. If eyes were the window to the soul, his eyes were inviting and made me feel safe. Neil kept his head bald and his face was framed by a well-manicured mustache and beard with nice, sensuous lips. Both forearms were covered with tattooed sleeves. When people looked at Neil, they saw a street-wise guy. But I knew he was soft on the inside.

I found a spot on Neil's Futon and curled up in a corner. I wrapped myself in his robe and he handed me a cup of tea. As Neil sat next to me on the futon, I uncurled my legs and rested them in his lap. Beginning to unwind, I started telling him about my dream. They all started off the same way. I can clearly see a girl in a field, but I cannot see her face. I can tell she's hot and tired. I can see the sweat running down her neck onto her dress. I can see the man, but I can't see his face. I can tell he's a white man. He's always mounted on a horse with his hat drawn low over his eyes. He has a rifle strapped to his back. In my dream, the girl is scared. I can feel her fear. I can feel her heart racing. I have always talked about these dreams with Neil until I get to the rape. It's almost as if I'm ashamed to talk about it even though it's a dream.

"Hmmm, so the same thing happens every time huh?" Neil asked while rubbing my feet.

"Yeah, that's what's bugging me. I didn't start having these dreams until I moved into Winston. I swear, the first week here.....Bamm! I

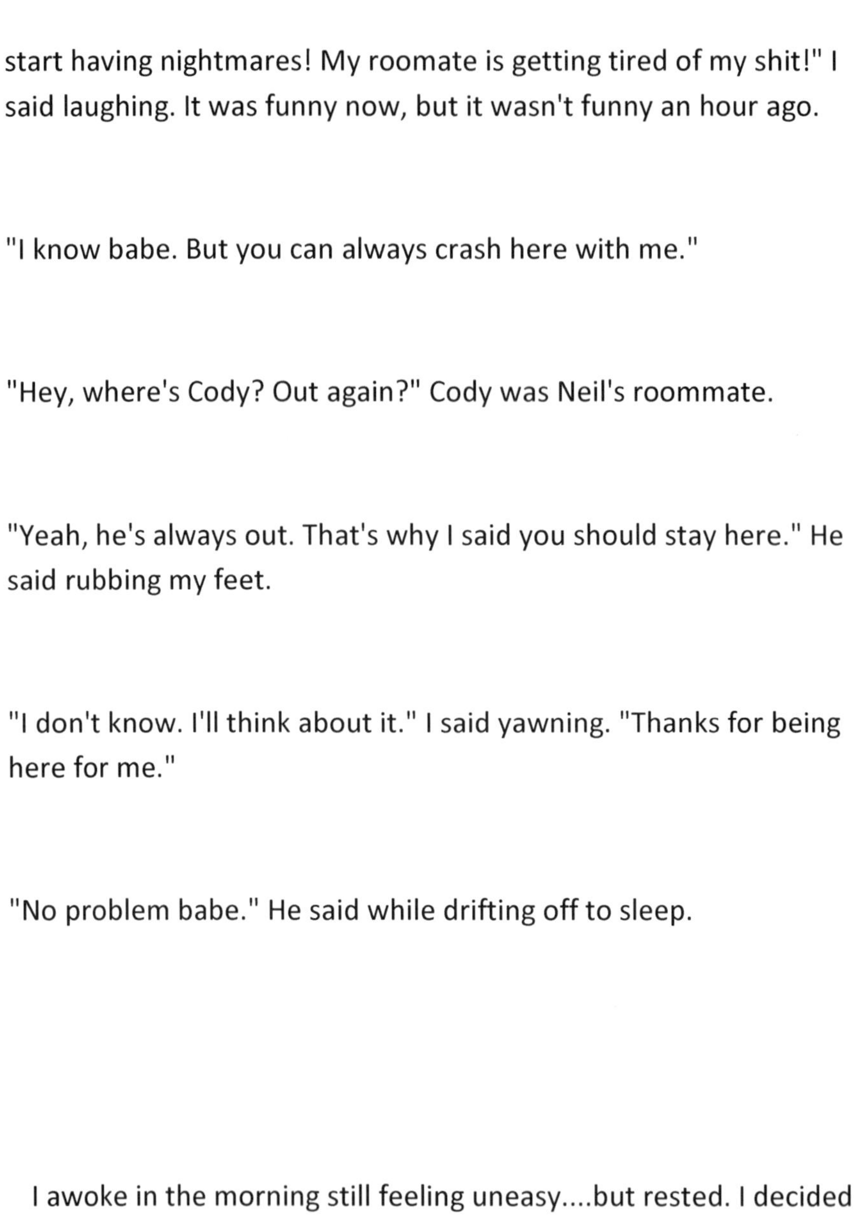

start having nightmares! My roomate is getting tired of my shit!" I said laughing. It was funny now, but it wasn't funny an hour ago.

"I know babe. But you can always crash here with me."

"Hey, where's Cody? Out again?" Cody was Neil's roommate.

"Yeah, he's always out. That's why I said you should stay here." He said rubbing my feet.

"I don't know. I'll think about it." I said yawning. "Thanks for being here for me."

"No problem babe." He said while drifting off to sleep.

I awoke in the morning still feeling uneasy....but rested. I decided to go for a run before class started. I slipped out, trying not to wake Neil. After showering and dressing, I headed out into the brisk morning air. I enjoyed spending time running in the morning. The campus was beautiful. I jogged at a steady pace along the pinewood trail at the end of the south campus. The trail was a good workout, filled with hills and bends. After awhile, all I could hear was the steady rhythm of my heart beat. After four miles, I turned to head back. I walked briskly along the trail. A small cabin nestled almost behind a couple of majestic trees caught my eye off to the left. I hadn't noticed it before. It was an old log cabin that looked as if it had been abandoned for years. After about ten minutes, I reached Winston Hall. I was exhausted, but energized as I climbed the three flights of stairs to get to my room. Lynn hadn't returned. *I guess she's still pissed*, I thought to myself smiling. I showered, dressed, and left to get something to eat before class.

I loved campus life in the fall. I looked forward to homecoming weekend and the parties. But I especially looked forward to spending time with my family for Thanksgiving back in Philly. Neil asked me to spend the holidays with his family this year, and of course I said yes. Now I have been trying to find a way to tell my folks I won't be coming to Thanksgiving dinner this year. They aren't going to be too happy about this news either. Mom and dad hosted Thanksgiving dinner for our entire family every year. It's our family's tradition. But I really wanted to meet Neil's parents. Besides, I'm curious to see what white people eat for Thanksgiving. Should be interesting. Just to be on the safe side, I'm bringing my own jar of Lawry's seasoning salt. I thought it was sweet of Neil to ask me to spend the holiday with him and his family. We've been getting pretty serious lately. We haven't exactly talked about an engagement or anything, but I think it's a huge deal for him to ask me to meet his folks. Maybe he can spend Christmas with me at my parents home. My mom and dad are the coolest parents ever, and I know that Neil would just love them the same way I do. My mom is a sweet lady with the sharpest tongue in town. She is notorious for throwing people out of our house on the holidays when she got tired. Everybody knew when Anna said get out, she meant it! And my dad.....what can I say? I have the best father in the world. My dad is one of those cool, laid-back type of guys. He served our Country as a Marine and is a fierce protector and provider of our family. My dad is the smartest man I know. He is a very deep thinker, especially after a round of medicinal "Mary Jane". My family is super open-minded. I know Neil will be welcomed with open arms for sure. After all, Leon and Anna did not play when it came to the happiness of me, my brothers, and my sisters. Well, I have three more weeks before the Thanksgiving break so I will try to slip it in the conversation with my mom the next time we talk.

CHAPTER-2

Neil was born and raised in Louisianna. His parents lived upstate. About two hours away from school. We planned to leave school at five in the morning and take the scenic route. I wanted to get in a little tour before heading to his parents' house. Neil is from a modest sized family. You know, the mother and father, sister and brother, and of course... the family pooch. Text book shit. Neil showed me pictures of his house and family on Facebook, and it was exactly what I had expected. Single home, large sprawling lawn with built-in sprinkler system, a few Oak trees lining the sidewalk, and a winding drive-way leading to the garage on the side of the house. Text book shit. Neil showed me the bedroom window that he used to sneak out of on Saturday nights to go to parties. He showed me a picture of his pristine mother, with her blonde hair pulled back tightly in a bun, and freshly manicured fingernails. I remember my mom used to always say " Ain't nobody got time for all that primpin', chile. He better like what he see!" Then I saw a picture of Neil's father. His hair was red and so was his neck. He looked tired and mean at the same damn time. The picture of Neil's dad made me feel uneasy. I asked Neil if he was sure it was okay for me to come. He reassured me that his folks would love me.

"Neil, just because you love me doesn't mean they will. Answer this....how many black friends do your parents have?" I asked, since that's the first thing white people use as proof they aren't racist.

"What!? Yo, you trippin'!" He said laughing.

"Okay, cut the 'black-lingo' cause you are not that cool." I said laughing. "Just answer the question. How many black friends do your parents have?"

"Shari, my parents have several black friends. But we don't call our friends 'friends'. We consider our friends extended family. Now how about you tell me how many white friends your parents have.....huh?"

"Come on Neil! Now you know! We have friends of all shapes, sizes, and colors! We live on a block full of different races. Shit, we have Poppi and them on one side and the Mclaughlins on the other, so please!" I said laughing. "Don't be mad because your ass was a sheltered little spoiled kid." I laughed while throwing my arms around his neck and kissing him on the cheek.

"Yeah, alright....I got your spoiled brat!" He said as he smacked me on the ass.

Our laughing slowly turned into passionate kisses. His lips were soft and his tongue was warm and probing. I wrapped my arms tighter around his neck and my legs around his waist as he lifted me up. His tongue was hungry for my mouth as we backed onto the bed. I could feel his hardness pulsating on my ass. Breathing became more heavy and labored as we lay on the bed. I couldn't wait for him to be inside, and he couldn't wait to get there. His mouth moved down to my neck where he swirled his tongue over every inch and traveled down to my breast. He squeezed them and let his tongue circle around the nipples. He slapped my ass firmly. I grabbed his throbbing hardness and guided it slowly inside. Our bodies became one, rhythmic, rocking motion, faster and harder with each stroke. My wetness soaked his thighs and I could feel him about to cum. "I love you bae." I whispered in his ear as we both erupted with intense orgasms and passionate moans. After, we

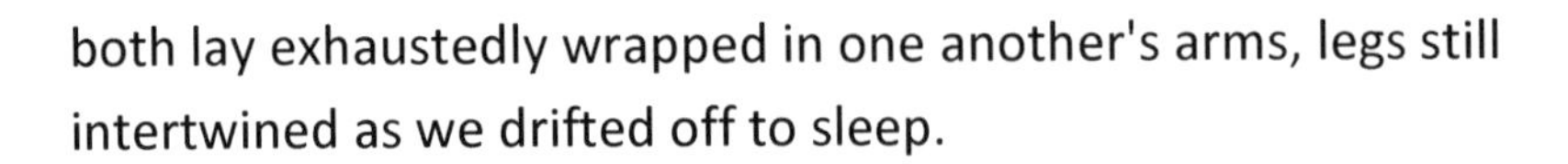

both lay exhaustedly wrapped in one another's arms, legs still intertwined as we drifted off to sleep.

****
****

Every thrust felt like a knife cutting deep into my flesh. I can see myself laying there on the muddy river bank. I looked dead, but I can feel every vile inch. I've learned to leave my body when this happens. He can have my body, but he can't have my soul. I can always tell when he's coming for me. I can see him watching me at the end of the field. I don't make eye contact. I just keep tending to the crops. I can feel him getting closer. I can smell the whiskey on him. I can see his fat, sweaty back humping on my lifeless body, and I wish I had a gun! I wish I had a gun so I could shoot him right in the ass! I want to swing my arms, but I can't move. I want to kick, but my legs are heavy as lead. I want to yell, but the sound is stuck in my throat. I want to scream! Scream damnit! Just fucking scream! SCREEAAAMMMMM!!

I was startled awake by Neil shaking me and shouting in my ear. I opened my eyes slowly and blinked a few times. What the fuck is going on?! The sheets were on the floor. Neil's looking at me wide-eyed. I unloosed myself from his grasp and rubbed my eyes to remove the blur, only to find my face wet. *Was I crying? Was I crying!?*

"Neil I'm sorry! I told you! These damn dreams are tripping me out!

"You scared the shit out of me! You were screaming and crying and I couldn't wake you up! I kept yelling your name, but you wouldn't stop! I shook your shoulders and you started swinging and kicking. You hit me in my lip!"

"Babe I'm sorry! That shit was scary! Feel my heart! It's still beating fast!" I said grabbing his hand and placing it on my chest.

"I'll get you some water."

I lay back down, trying to make sense of things. I remembered some things. That poor girl! She's young, even though I can't see her face. She must be about 13 or 14-years old. And I want to kill that fucking bastard! I'm angry, but afraid at the same time. I'm scared for the girl, but I'm scared for myself too. There was something menacing about that man. I couldn't see his face, but there was something very evil.......and soulless about that man! Neil came back with the water and I took a sip.

"Why do I keep having these dreams?"

"Babe, either you're stressed from classes and midterms, or maybe it's from extreme exhaustion."

"That could be true....but shit! If it's exhaustion, it's these fucking dreams that's causing it!" I said laughing.

"You know what Shari, maybe it's guilt manifested by the fact that you think you're going to let your parents down when you tell them you're not coming home for Thanksgiving. I'm sure it's something like that. Hey, why don't you call your mom in the morning and just tell her? Just get it out of the way. I bet those dreams will stop!"

Neil talked me into agreeing to tell my mom in the morning. He fixed the sheets and we lay back down. I snuggled against his chest and tried to forget about the dream.

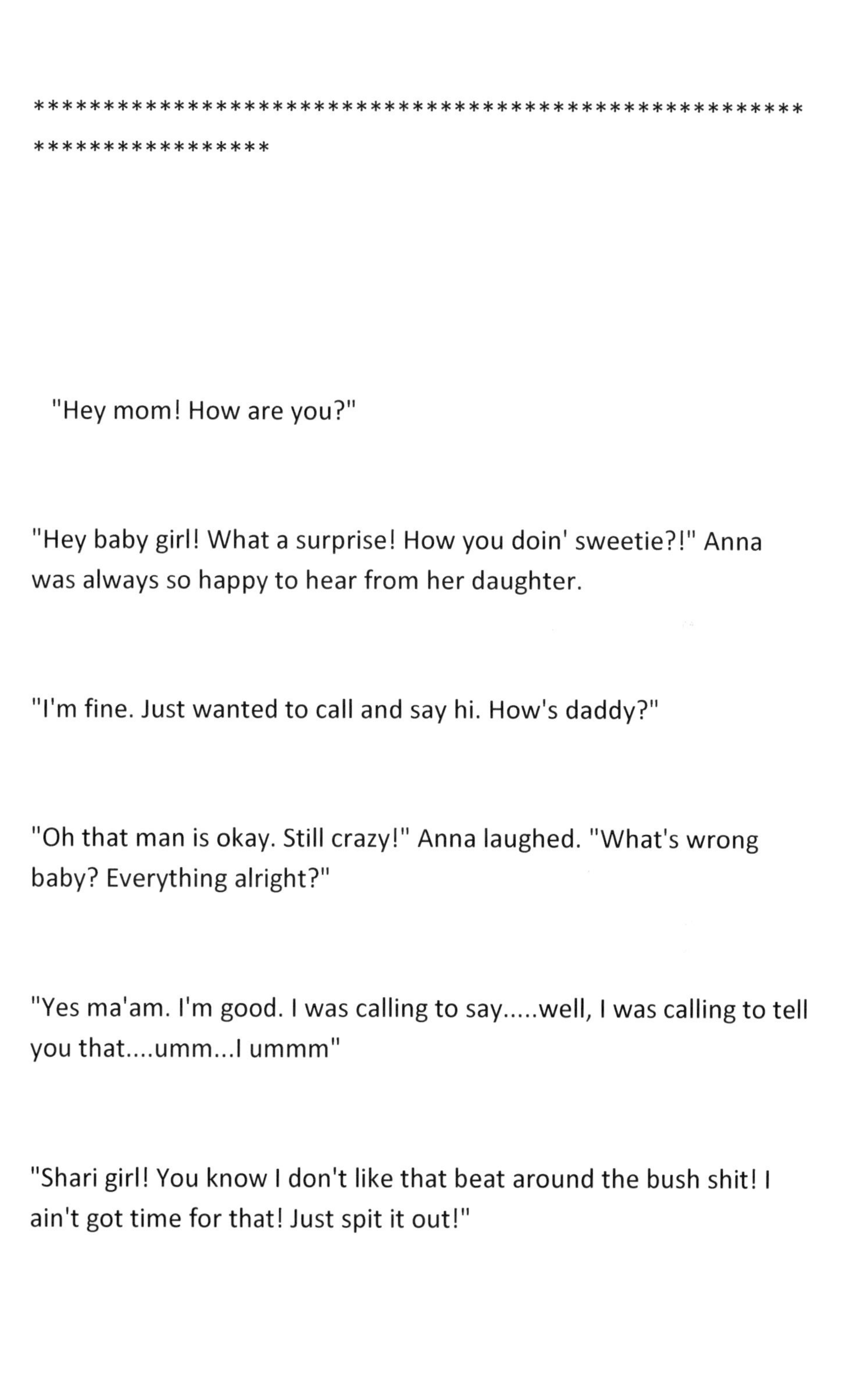

****
****

"Hey mom! How are you?"

"Hey baby girl! What a surprise! How you doin' sweetie?!" Anna was always so happy to hear from her daughter.

"I'm fine. Just wanted to call and say hi. How's daddy?"

"Oh that man is okay. Still crazy!" Anna laughed. "What's wrong baby? Everything alright?"

"Yes ma'am. I'm good. I was calling to say.....well, I was calling to tell you that....umm...I ummm"

"Shari girl! You know I don't like that beat around the bush shit! I ain't got time for that! Just spit it out!"

"Okay, okay! Sheesh, you're so rude!" I said laughing. "Mom, I'm going to spend Thanksgiving with Neil and his family this year....you okay with that?"

"Well, what do you expect for me to say? No, you can't go? Shari, you are 21-years old. I raised you right and I trust you. We'll miss you, but this is your life sweetheart. You go and have a good time."

"Mom, one more thing, Neil is.....umm.....a little light skinned." I said laughing.

"Well what's so funny about that? That other thing you used to date was damn near albino."

"No mom, I mean Neil is white."

"And?!" My mom and that tongue of hers again.

"Nothing. I just though I'd let you know."

"Oh okay. Just make sure you take your own jar of Lawry's when you go." Anna said laughing.

"Alright mommy!" I said laughing before we exchanged "I love you's" and hung up.

CHAPTER-3

November 17, 1810

The points and splinters of the tree bark pressed firmly into my flesh, *almost threatening to break the skin. I don't care, because if it wasn't for me hugging this tree, I would surely be on my knees, and then my face by now. I squeezed hold of the tree with all my might, gripping tighter with every lashing of his whip. I think I counted seven, but I keep slipping in and out of awareness. My body is numb with pain. I can feel the warmth of the blood trickling from my back down to my ass. Massa Willis begins to huff out of breath* *and I know he's going to quit soon. I just hold on tight to this tree real hard and close my eyes real tight.*

"One of you niggers get this wench and clean her up! Now!" Massa Willis yelled out of breath. I guess he mad cause Miss Sarah caught him on top of me. Miss Sarah was awful mad at Massa Willis. She say he fuck dirty niggers and mess up her clean sheets when he come to bed. She said she never sleep with him again unless he sell me. Massa beat me instead. Like it was my fault. I guess it satisfied Miss Sarah some, because she went back to her needle point as if nothing ever happened. I'm not the only person Massa Willis have sex with. One late night I was out back looking for some Aloe to make an ointment. I heard noise in the outhouse. I snuck closer. I saw Massa Willis and the new Irish slave boy, Jimmy. Jimmy was doing to Massa what Massa do to me! Jimmy was behind Massa and Massa Willis was jus' a' moanin' and groanin'. I wonder how Miss Sarah would feel about Massa getting fucked by a dirty Paddy boy? I think Massa would fuck the barnyard animals if he could.

Ms. Hattie helped me up from the ground after I let loose the tree. Mr. Jasper, who tends the horses, helped carry me to the slave cabin. Ms. Hattie and Mr. Jasper belonged to Massa Willis daddy before he died. The two were like a momma and poppa to me now, since my own family was gone.

"Savannah chile, why you make Massa so mad I will never know!" Ms Hattie whispered as she cleaned my back. I winced in pain, a

tear trickling down my face. Ms. Hattie put a clean wrapping on my back.

"Ms. Hattie, if I don't get away from here, Massa is bound to kill me!" I whispered exhaustedly, shivering from the pain.

"Chile, you just gotta pray and stay out of his sight! Just stay out of his sight!"

"But Ms. Hattie, I works in Massa house! In his kitchen! Oh Ms. Hattie, what I's gonna do!?"

Mr. Jasper stood from his chair and chimed in, "Savannah gal, you listen to me! You gonna hafta kill Massa before he kill you! You let God worry about your soul later!" Mr. Jasper turned away, limping towards the door.

****

Neil and I spent the entire evening after classes packing and planning our visit to his parents' house. I am a little nervous. I want to impress his folks, and I want them to know that I'm good for their son. Neil is such a great guy. He's a good son and a good person. I could go as far as to say he's one of my biggest supporters. He's my best friend, and I know I can tell him anything. I can't seem to figure out why I can't tell him the intimate details of my dreams. I feel ashamed every time I recount the things I dream. I will tell him one day, but right now, I just want to be dream-free and enjoy time getting to know his folks.

"Babe, we're only staying two nights! Why do you have two suitcases?" Neil said flopping down on the bed. He leaned back on his elbows and smiled.

"Well, you never know what a girl might need on any given day! See....this dress is for a casual evening. And this one is just in case we do something formal. Goodness Neil, get with the program!" I laughed and threw the dresses back in the bag. "Oh, and this little number here....this is just in case your parents leave us alone in the house!"

"Girl, you are too much! I love you Shar." Neil said as he stood and pulled me close. He kissed me softly.

"I love you too babe. So, what time should we leave in the morning?"

"I don't know? About six? Sound good to you?"

"Yup, I'm exhausted!" I said yawning. "I think I'm going to bed in a few. I'm going to read a little and then I'm shutting these eyes. Can I crash with you tonight?"

"Of course! How the hell else are you going to get up so early?!" Neil said laughing.

I showered and threw on one of Neil's T-shirts and my boy shorts. I wrapped my braids in a bun and tied a scarf around my head. I grabbed my book from my backpack and climbed into bed next to Neil. I loved curling up next to his warm body at night. He always made me feel safe at night. As much as I would've loved to nestle and snuggle in his arms, I had to get a jump on my African-American history assignment due after the break. I opened the massive hard-cover text book and flipped through the pages. I liked books with pictures, and this book had loads of old photos. I'm no history buff, but I do think that it's so cool the way historians piece together time periods with pictures and stories. I'm also not good with remembering dates, so this is going to be tough. As I flipped through the pages, I came across a picture that stopped me from turning. The cabin! I read the small caption under the picture: { *Slave Quarters; circa 1810* } A row of small log cabins with narrow doorways and squared windows on each side of the door. Behind the cabins was a forest and a small stream. The photo was black and white, but the longer I gazed, the more vivid the colors became. The grass in the picture slowly turned green and the cabin brown. The plantation house that sat in the distance, red brick with white frames. The sky above turned blue. I couldn't turn away. It felt so familiar. *I can feel the cool breeze blowing as I watch the leaves fly in a circular motion, as if dancing to the song of the winds. I walk along the pathway between the cabins, my bare feet making the leaves crunch beneath my steps. I walk toward the cabin. It's calling me, pulling me, pushing me. I stop at the steps of the cabin. I lift my leg to begin the climb up the stairs. My hand holding the narrow railing. I take a step on the stairs. Hot! I can feel a sharp pain behind me! A painful heat!*

"Shari! Shari!" Neil said loudly, startling me. I jumped, and the book fell to the floor.

"What!? You scared me!"

"Turn out the light babe! You're snoring! Get some sleep."

Confused and a little shaken, I shut the light and laid down on my side, resting my head on my forearm. "*Sleeping? But I was wide awake!*" I thought as I began to drift off.

CHAPTER-4

Neil and I woke early to get going on our trip. We put our suitcases in the car and checked for any last minute things we might need along the way. We would grab coffee along the way. I started changing into my sweatshirt and tights for the ride. As I slipped the sweatshirt above my head I felt a sharp pain.

"Ouch! My back really hurts!" I said trying to look at the painful area in the mirror.

"Let me see." Neil said pulling up my shirt. "I don't see anything. Oh, wait, bend over a little toward the light." Neil said running his hand along my side. He got closer. "Looks like a bite or something. You probably slept on top of something. Or maybe a coil from the mattress was pressed into your side. Wow! This really looks like a bite mark! Like a human bite....look right here! That looks like the upper teeth mark. And here's the lower." He said rubbing as if to wipe it away.

I laughed a little. "It sure does! You're so silly Neil. I probably slept on something. Hey, we'd better get going. Road Trippppp!!!" I said, grabbing my bag. The thought of what could have bitten me on my back unnerved me some, but I pushed it to the back of my mind. I wasn't going to mess up our fun with my dumb superstitious beliefs.

The Louisianna countryside was magnificent. I absolutely love the fall and the changing colors of the landscape. The clusters of red, orange, and brown leaves hung loosely on their branches. The trees lined both sides of the road as if to stand guarding the forest. There was a crisp coolness in the air, but the sun was shining brightly and warmed my face as I looked up at the sky. I lazily hung my arm on the back of Neil's seat, kicked off my sneakers, and tucked one leg under the other as I made myself comfortable. Neil and I liked to do "car karaoke" and he was already in full swing, rapping *Bad and Boujee.* I just watched and smiled. He is so funny and goofy! He is a big hip-hop fan. I turned and stared out the window. *What the fuck is this mark on my side?!* It's so peaceful watching nature pass us by as we drive along. I looked back over at Neil and he's still going at it.

I laughed inside. He knows how to entertain himself. In a few minutes he's going to require that I take a turn. He makes me so happy! *Could this be a human bite mark for real?!*

After two hours, and one pee stop, we arrived at Neil's parents' house. We barely got to the end of the driveway before the front door of the house swung open. Letting out a barking, flappy eared dog, followed by a short, red-haired woman wearing a white button-down shirt, blue jeans, and a pair of white Keds on her feet. Her hair was pulled back into a bun. She stood at the end of the driveway wiping her hands on the apron tied around her waist. We parked and got out of the car. I grabbed one of my bags in an effort to delay being first to leave the car.

"Hey ma!" Neil greeted his mother with a kiss on the cheek.

"Oh, hi son!" Mrs. Mcgee said hugging her son tight and patting his back. "How've you been? Are you eating? Ya' hungry? I just started a pot of soup! Oh, and this is your friend...Charlotte?"

"That's Shari ma!" Neil said and chuckled.

"Hello ma'am. It's nice to meet you." I said, sticking my hand out for a shake. Mrs. Mcgee grabbed my hand and pulled me in for a hug.

"Well hello Shari! It's so nice to finally meet you and put a face to the name! How are you honey? Ya' hungry? You two come on in here and I'll get you something to drink. Neil, go get the bags out of the car! Come with me Shari! I know you probably have to use the little girl's room by now!" Mrs Mcgee was a ball of energy. She was bossy too!

Neil bought our luggage into the house and sat next to me on the couch. Mrs. Mcgee had poured us a few glasses of iced tea and had pulled out the old family photo album. I sipped my tea and looked over at Neil, just in time to see the look of horror and pain on his face when he noticed the books. I laughed a little and cleared my throat to muffle the laugh.

"Oh Neil, don't be afraid! You had a cute little butt-butt when you were a baby!" His mother said teasingly. We laughed as we went through each photo. Mrs. Mcgee had a story about each one of them. She was a proud, family woman. She spoke highly about each member of her family. As we flipped through the pages of their family history, one of the pictures fell on the floor. I bent to pick it up and glared at it while it lay on the floor. I picked it up slowly, staring intently.

"Mrs. Mcgee, who is this?" I asked almost in a whisper.

"Let me see that? Oh, this is Neil's great-great pawpaw Tomas. Pawpaw Tomas was one of our family's first settlers down here. Hey, did Neil tell ya? Pawpaw owned that land where the University sits today! Yup, he was filthy rich and owned over 20 slaves...."

"Ma!" Neil interrupted. His face was turning as red as a beet. Whatever his mother was about to say, he made sure to cut her off. "Uh, what time is pop coming home? We're hungry. Is he going to be much longer?"

"Umm...well, no honey. He should be home soon. Why don't you and Shari go on up to your roon and get rested before dinner." Mrs. Mcgee said gathering the photos from the coffee table.

Neil and I headed upstairs to his bedroom. I lay across the bed and watched Neil walk over to the window and stare.

"What's wrong Neil? Your mom didn't do anything wrong. I just asked who the man in the picture was. How much do you know about him? He looks like he was a real sonofabitch. Neil....Neil?"

"I'm listening babe. I'm sorry. I just hate when she starts with those fucking old pictures."

"Why? All parents do that! It's not embarrassing!"

"Well, it's embarrassing when you know for a fact that your ancestors owned slaves! I hate that shit! My ma....see....sometimes she forgets who she's talking to, she talks so much! One time, we went to this Chinese restaurant to celebrate my Pop's birthday and she says to the waiter, pointing at another guest, *'Is that one of your relatives? Ya'll look so much alike!'* Like, what the fuck, Shar!? Yo, she can be embarrassing sometimes! I just don't want her to mess up what we have." Neil turned back towards the window.

I got up and walked over to him. I put my arms around his waist and laid my head on his back. "It's okay baby. She can't scare me off. But why didn't you tell me you guys own the college!?"

"We don't own the school. The land belonged to the family. And I didn't mention it because....well....because it used to be a plantation and shit! Pawpaw's plantation. Listen, Shari, I don't really want to talk about this, okay?"

"Okay, okay. We don't have to talk about it. But you better not leave me alone with your parents! I don't want to have to curse a bitch out!" I said laughing.

Later that evening, Neil's father came home. Neil introduced us. He was nice enough, kind of quiet. We had dinner. Mrs Mcgee did most of the talking. Neil was right, she sure did talk a lot about nothing. Neil's father mostly just nodded his head or made small comments about whatever she was talking about.

"So Shari, where about are you from?" Mr. Mcgee asked in the middle of taking a bite of his steak.

"We live in Philadelphia, sir. I don't know if you know about the different parts of Philly, but we live in the Northeast part of Philly." I said after swallowing my sip of tea.

"Oh yeah? Is that close to downtown Philadelphia?" He asked.

"No sir. It's actually about 30 minutes away from Center City. Well, 30 minutes driving that is. It's a really nice neighborhood."

"Ahhh I see. So, Shari, what does your folks do for a living?" He asked. I knew that question was coming! It was only a matter of time, but I knew it was coming! I wanted to say *well my father is the leader of The Black Panthers and my mom turns tricks on the side to help feed us!*

"My father is a State Representative and my mother manages our home."

"So she's unemployed huh?"

"Well no....she's not unemployed...sir. She's a housewife whose husband earns a very decent salary, so she doesn't need to work. My mother has been married to my father for over 25 years. My father who takes very, very, good care of my family and his home. So, no, she's not unemployed. She has no need to work outside of the home. My mom says her job is her family, so....yeah.....I guess that's that....sir." I saw where this shit was going. I saw all types of stereotypes starting to play out in this man's head.

Neil interrupted, "Hey, what is this? Jeopardy?" Neil and I made eye contact. He could tell that I was gearing up for battle. He rubbed my knee under the table and returned to the conversation with his father. The evening ended awkwardly. Afterwards, we headed outside for a night stroll. Hand in hand we walked and talked. Neil pointed out the trees he used to climb, the house that always managed to get in the way of his football tossing, and the many lawns he had to cut during the summer months to earn money. It was at that moment I felt the most secure with him that I wanted to share the intimate details about my dreams. I told him about the white man in my dreams that sits on a horse, hat drawn low over his eyes, holding a rifle. I told about how my heart races every time I saw this man, or sensed his presence. I told him about the girl who I felt a connection with and how I could feel her fear. I could feel her anger. I could feel her pain. Finally, I told him about the many times I saw this man raping this girl. Over and over and over!

"But Shari, it's just a dream. You think you can feel stuff, but it's just a dream babe."

"I know, I know! It's supposed to be a dream, but I'm telling you, I can feel it! I didn't want to tell you because I don't want you to think I'm crazy, but I can really feel....whatever that girl feels! Remember that bite mark you saw on my side? Well, I dreamt about the girl, right. She was washing clothes in a stream and I could feel the man standing behind her. When she looked up, he was there. He punched her in the face. When she fell back, he was on top of her, ripping at her clothes, scratching her thighs trying to pry them open." My eyes began to tear up. "He was on her, crushing her! I could feel her heart pounding in her chest and mine! She fought from under him and tried to run, but he grabbed her ankle. When she fell, he bit her! He bit her hard on her back! He raped her and left her there, lying in mud and leaves." I was fully sobbing by now. "Why would someone do something like that!? Neil, she's a kid! She's a little kid! No more than 13 or 14-years old!"

Neil held me close and rubbed my back. He kept assuring me that it was okay and it was just a dream.

CHAPTER-5

December 12, 1810....

Massa Willis hate me. *I can see it in his eyes every time he look at me. I try to stay out of his way. I even asked to work in the* *fields with Ms. Hattie so I don't have to be in that house. That house is filled with evil! Massa fucking Jimmy. Jimmy fucking Ms. Sarah. The last day I worked in that house, I was scrubbing floors on the first floor. I could hear Ms. Sarah moaning Jimmy's name, and the bed's headboard banging against the wall. I was so scared Massa Willis was going to come in and kill all of us! But he didn't. Now I work in the fields. I don't worry as much, unless Massa come out to see what we doin'. I don't worry, cause I's got a plan. Tomorrow, after supper, after Massa drunk and passed out, I'm running away! I just need to make it to the river bank at the edge of the northeast forest. Mr. Jasper know a man that help slaves escape. He said he would have a boat waitin' for me. I'm not takin' nothin' but the clothes on my back. I plan to head up North to Philadelphia. I knows my momma and poppa there.*

Me, momma, poppa, my little brother Benny, and my sister Nettie, we all lived right here on Massa Willis' plantation when Massa's father was still alive. Massa's father was mean, but not as mean as Massa Willis. Massa's father never harmed us slaves. Momma and poppa was Massa's best slaves. When Massa's father died, Massa Willis started drinking a lot. He would get drunk and try to get my momma or me alone. Poppa said we would have to leave this place before he hurt us. Mr. Jasper and poppa made plans for us to leave one night with Mr. Jasper's help. Mr. Jasper know people who could help us escape. Momma told me to leave everything and just take the small stuff I needed. I was nervous all that day. I tried to act normal. I helped Ms. Sarah with the wash and cleared the dishes after dinner for Massa and the kids. I headed back to our cabin after, just like momma told me. I went to the cabin and started stuffing all the things I loved in my dress pockets. Most importantly, I grabbed my ivory hair pendant grandma gave to me before she died. She say it came straight from Senegambia, our Mother Land in Africa. It had been passed down from her grandma to her momma, and from her momma to her.

Mr. Jasper told poppa that once the moon had risen high above the sky and dew set on the grass, one by one we should make our way down to the river bank. Momma didn't want to go without us kids, but poppa assured her that we would be okay. We would know what to do. So, momma tucked us into bed to act like we was sleeping until the time was right. Once the moon rose high and the dew moistened the grass, poppa woke us up. One by one we left the cabin. Giving each other time to put distance in-between. Momma went first as poppa instructed. Then my sister, then my brother. Only me and poppa remained. Poppa told me to go next. He wanted to be last so he could be sure that everyone else got out safely. I ran with every bit of strength I had. I jumped the high grass and ducked the tree branches. My heart pounded in my chest. If Massa caught us he would do horrible things to momma and poppa. He would sell me, my sister, and brother. I ran by the light of the moon as fast as I could. I ran through a thick brush of tree roots and my foot became tangled. I fell hard. Everything in my pockets fell out. I frantically unloosed my foot and began to search for grandma's Ivory hair pendant. With outstretched hands, I searched blindly in the dark.

My fingers were getting cut from the thorny brush roots. My heart was racing. My head was spinning. Poppa gon' be mad! Momma gon' scold me good!

As I searched for the pendant, I heard barking dogs and hollering men approaching. I laid low and tried to cover myself in the brush. The sounds became closer. I could see a shadow run by. It was poppa! I wanted to call for help! I wanted him to help me! I wanted to run with him! Minutes later, more shadows. Massa Willis and his farm-hand with their dogs. But poppa had a large lead and was a distance away. I guess Massa and the farm-hand got tired, because they slowed down and turned back. Suddenly they stopped. They turned back and the dogs started barking. They were headed my way! They were coming for me! They let the dogs loose and they ran right to me. They bit me all over my arms and legs. Massa watched for what felt like forever before he pulled them off. I was dragged back to the cabin and repeatedly beaten and raped until Massa fall asleep. The next morning I woke. Ms. Hattie was cleaning and bandaging my bite wounds. Ms. Hattie had taken the role of momma for the past three years, but I wanted my real momma! I wanted my real poppa!

So now, when I tell Ms. Hattie my plans to run again, she slapped me hard in the face. "Chile! You gonna get us all killed! Don't you know when Massa find you ran, he gonna whip us all!?" Ms. Hattie spewed through clenched teeth.

"Ms Hattie, I's gotta go! I can't stay here no longer! Massa hate me! I can see it in his eyes! It's a matter of time before he get me!" I yelled. "I ain't got nobody, Ms. Hattie! No momma and no poppa! I know they up North somewhere! I gotta find my family Ms. Hattie! Every time Massa rape me, he killin' me slow. He killin' me little by little." I said crying.

Ms. Hattie put her hand on my shoulder and pulled me in for a hug. Tomorrow night would change everything!

CHAPTER-6

Thanksgiving at Neil's house was interesting, to say the least. Most of his family were very kind. His father made me uncomfortable though. I would occasionally catch him staring at me from the corner of the room. Neil tried to dismiss it due to his drinking, but I felt it was more personal than that. Since we've been back to campus, I've tried to ask more about Neil's connection with the University, but he shuts me down. The fact that his family owned slaves really upset him. Before we leave for winter break, I'm going to do a little research of my own. I love Neil, but he can be so stubborn at times! I'll just go around him. Besides, my dreams have become more intense since we've been back. Neil keeps suggesting "I go talk to someone", code for "go see a shrink". I probably should. The last dream I had was the most violent.

The young girl was in a field. Her forehead was sweaty. I can tell she's been working hard. That man was staring at her from his horse, hat pulled low over his eyes. The girl's thin cotton dress is sticking to her from sweat, making it easy to see the form of her body. The dress was wedged into her backside when she bent down and stood up. That man is watching her as he spits out chewing tobacco. He calls for her to go get him water from the nearby stream. She doesn't want to go alone. She ask if one of the field hands can go with her. He tells her no. As she slowly walks into the woods to get to the stream, she can feel him following close behind. His horse's hooves kicks leaves as it slowly gallops along. She continues to the stream. Once there, he dismounts his horse. She slowly turns to ask him, what to put the water in? He backhands her hard. Her lip is split and bleeding. She begins to sob and back away. He grabs her arm and tosses her to the ground. He begins to kick her before falling to his knees to punch her. He punches her until she passes out.

The next day when I woke, I had a cut on my lip and my ribs were bruised and sore. I quickly realized, what was happening to the girl in my dreams could potentially kill me in real life! I've been terrified to sleep since then. I've also been staying at Neil's room every night since then. In his arms, I think I am safe. I tried to explain to Neil that what happened to my lip, happened to the girl in my dream. He wants to believe me, and he believes that I fully believe, but he just can't understand.

Later that evening, I went to the library to do a little research on the University. Louisianna University was built in 1812 after purchasing the land from a tobacco plantation. The widow of the plantation sold the land to Sir Randall Scott, because she couldn't keep up with the land or the many slaves they owned. The widow, Ms. Sarah Willis, died soon after selling the land and the slaves. I went to do a search of Sarah Willis and found that she was the wife of prominent businessman, Tomas Willis. Tomas Willis owned over 20 slaves and had a thriving tobacco plantation. In 1810, Tomas Willis was killed by one of his slaves. The report said that his head was bashed in so badly, they couldn't immediately identify him. It was only after his wife reported him missing for three days, that the authorities realized it was him. My heart was pounding! I called Mrs. Mcgee.

"Hi honey! How are you doing? It was so nice to meet you last month!" Mrs Mcgee answered the phone excitedly. "How's my boy doing? You taking care of him?"

"Hi Mrs Mcgee. Yes, Neil is fine. Mrs. Mcgee, I need to ask you a question."

"Go on hun."

"Um, remember when we were looking through your photo album? And we came across that one picture, and you started to tell me about Neil's pawpaw? Can you finish? I mean, what were you going to say about him?"

"Oh hun, Neil is going to kill me!" She said laughing.

"No, it's okay! Really! I won't even tell him we talked. It's just that....um....I have this final report I'm working on, and it's about the history of the school, and I just thought, well, you being a part of history and everything, I could get some real info straight from the source."

"Oh! Okay, I see!" She said with a chuckle. "Well, Neil's pawpaw was a mean son-of-a-bitch, from the family stories. Kind of like Neil's dad. Neil's pawpaw owned slaves and was rich as crude oil, but stingy as a miser! After he died, his wife died and the University was built there. They didn't even clean it up much. Just plopped the building over top of everything. Neil hates that story, but it's the truth. Did that help?"

"Yes ma'am. Thanks for sharing that with me. I think I can wrap my report up now. Oh, but wait! What was his name.....pawpaw?"

"Oh, his name was Tomas. Tomas Willis."

My heart was pounding. My head began to spin.

I waited for Neil outside of his class to tell him what I had found out. After giving him all the information and details I'd found, he was speechless. I don't think he was prepared for what I told him.

"Babe, I think that man in my dreams is Tomas Willis! Your pawpaw Willis! I've been having these dreams so much now that I feel like I know him! And somebody killed him! On his plantation!"

"Okay, so if this is true, what now? Why now?" Neil said. "Shar, look babe, I love you. I don't want this messing up our thing, okay? Okay?"

"Neil it won't! I don't feel any differently about you! I just need to know why this is happening!" I said. "Maybe if the girl in my dreams kills him, or gets away, this will be over with. Then it will all stop!"

CHAPTER-7

The next morning I was up early for my run. I threw on a t-shirt and yoga pants. I slept for a total of two hours last night. I was afraid to fall into any kind of deep sleep. I didn't want the girl to come. I didn't want the terrifying man to come. I just didn't want to dream about anything. I stretched, and started my run. The air was crisp as I inhaled, exhaling puffs of breath. I ran along the pinewood trail. I was always guaranteed a good run with all of the hills and bends along the way. As I ran, my mind began to clear and my steps formed a rhythm with the beat of my heart. A mile and a half into my run, the cabin that I saw weeks ago caught my eye. My pace began to slower and I found myself leaving the trail. My jog became a slow walk. My breathing deepened as I got closer. I could hear the leaves crunch under each step. Sweat began to trickle down my forehead and temple. The cabin! The cabin felt familiar. I walked up to the slanted wooden stairs slowly. Two stairs were missing. I could see the grass beneath. The small porch was worn from the weather and the roof was caved-in. I wanted to go inside. Something was pulling me to go inside. My heart pounded in my chest and my breath quickened. I placed my hand on the splintered railing and stepped on the first step. Two stairs in the middle were missing, so I stepped over the hole to step on the top stair. As I stepped on the stair, it began to crack and give to my weight. My leg scraped the cracked wood as I began to fall to the ground under the stairs. The sharp edge of the racked wood sliced my leg from the knee to the lower shin. My head hit the bottom step and everything went black.

I awoke after what felt like minutes, but it was now night. *How long had I been out?* I gathered myself and began to stand. I was in lots of pain, and my leg was wet with blood and throbbing. I rubbed the back of my head. It was also wet with blood. I began to straighten my clothes, which was now a blue cotton dress instead of the t-shirt and yoga pants I had been wearing. My head was in a haze and my vision was blurry. I had to get back home! I know they're worried about me! I'm going to be in big trouble! Massa

Willis is going to whip me for this! My leg throbbed in pain with each step I took. My mind was in and out of distortion. *Are these cabins or trees lining the path?* I found my way back to the trail. I can see home in the clearing. I hobbled upstairs to my dorm room and opened the door. Exhausted and in pain, I slumped onto the bed and lay on my back. Fear took over my senses. I was immediately scared. I scrambled off the bed as I remembered I had to run! I had to get away! North! Where momma and poppa was! I started searching the room for my most valuable possessions that I could easily carry and slip into my dress while running. I grabbed my grandma's hair ornament, momma's gold necklace, and the 9" sewing shears to cut the thick brush roots so I don't get caught up this time. I heard someone coming to the door! It gotta be Massa! He knows! He knows I'm going to run away!

Shari ducked behind the side of the bed as the door swung open.

"Shari, what happened?! Where've you been!? I called campus security to look for you." *Neil yelled after seeing the muddy, blood soaked t-shirt Shari was wearing.*

"Massa Willis! I...I'm sorry! I went down to the stream and must've lost track of time! Please Massa! I'm sorry!"

"What?...What the fuck are you talking about? Shari, what happened!? Babe, come on, we need to get you to the hospital! You're bleeding!"

"No! No! PLEASE MASSA! STAY AWAT FROM ME! PLEASE!!! DON'T HURT ME!!!"

Neil walked closer to Shari to try to grab hold of her and take her to the hospital. As he reached out to grab her arm, Shari began wildly swinging the shears.

"NO! NO MORE! YOU WILL NEVER HURT ME AGAIN! NO! NOT AGAIN! NOT AGAIN!"

In a blind fury, Shari swung the shears until she was exhausted and out of breath. She collapsed on the floor. Breathing heavily, she slowly turned over on her back and let the shears slide from her hand. Her mind raced. She needed to escape. She would run up North and finally try to find her momma and poppa! She needed to go find Ms. Hattie first, and tell her what she'd done. She sat up and began to look around. The room spun in slow motion. The dresser, the desk with table top lamp, the books and papers haphazardly thrown on the floor, the bed, and Neil lying in a pool of blood. His body lay slumped over at the foot of the bed. Shari let out an anguished scream! A scream that birthed the pain that she would be feeling for a long time to come. The pain of one soul that helped free another soul.

"NEEEIIILLLL! OH GOD! NEEEIILLL!" *Shari sobbed, slowly crawling to his body. She lifted his head and cradled it in her lap. Neil's throat had been slashed and cut deeply. He made a low, barely audible, gurgling sound.*

"DOWN ON THE FLOOR!" *Campus cops came running into the room yelling. Shari rocked back and forth with Neil's head resting in her lap. She slowly looked up, tears streaming.*

"I don't know what happened. I....I don't know." *she whispered as she quietly sobbed.*

York Bound Publications

Presents:

SHARI'S CROSSING

Written by: R.D. ARCHER

Follow RD ARCHER on Twitter @Passion082

Follow York Bound Publications on Twitter @yorkboundpub

YORK BOUND PUBLICATIONS

Made in the USA
Middletown, DE
04 September 2021